D0516467

THE GREAT DICTIONARY CAPER

For Bob, my special pal(indrome)
—J. S.

To my mom and dad for encouraging me to follow my dreams.
"Hey look, Mom, I illustrated this book!"
—E. C.

SIMON & SCHUSTER BOOKS FOR YOUNG READERS
An imprint of Simon & Schuster Children's Publishing Division
1230 Avenue of the Americas, New York, New York 10020

Book design by Eric Comstock
The text for this book was set in Futura.
The illustrations for this book were rendered digitally.
Manufactured in China
1117 SCP
First Edition
2 4 6 8 10 9 7 5 3 1
CIP data for this title is available from the Library of Congress.
ISBN 978-1-4814-8004-8 (hc)
ISBN 978-1-4814-8005-5 (eBook)

THE GREAT DICTIONARY

WRITTEN BY JUDY SIERRA ILLUSTRATED BY ERIC COMSTOCK

A Paula Wiseman Book
Simon & Schuster Books for Young Readers
New York London Toronto Sydney New Delhi

This story is brought to you by Noah Webster and his amazing dictionary.

READY
SET
GO
WEBSTER'S
DICTIONARY

Words can get bored. They sit in the dictionary, day in, day out. It's time for a break.

LEXI-CON LOVES
Vocabulary
one
ride
GO

The **WORD PARADE** is about to begin, led by the onomatopoeia marching band.

Boom
mm
mmmmmmmmmmm
Tweedle
Bang
BEEP!
onk

Here come
the grand marshals:
that SELF-CENTERED
ONE-LETTER word

and everyone's favorite 34-LETTER word:

Jum
Bounce
run
Somersault

Action verbs
LOVE to show off.

The no-action contractions **NEED SOME HELP.**

I can't
didn't
don't

Homophones
tango
TWO by TWO
EYE

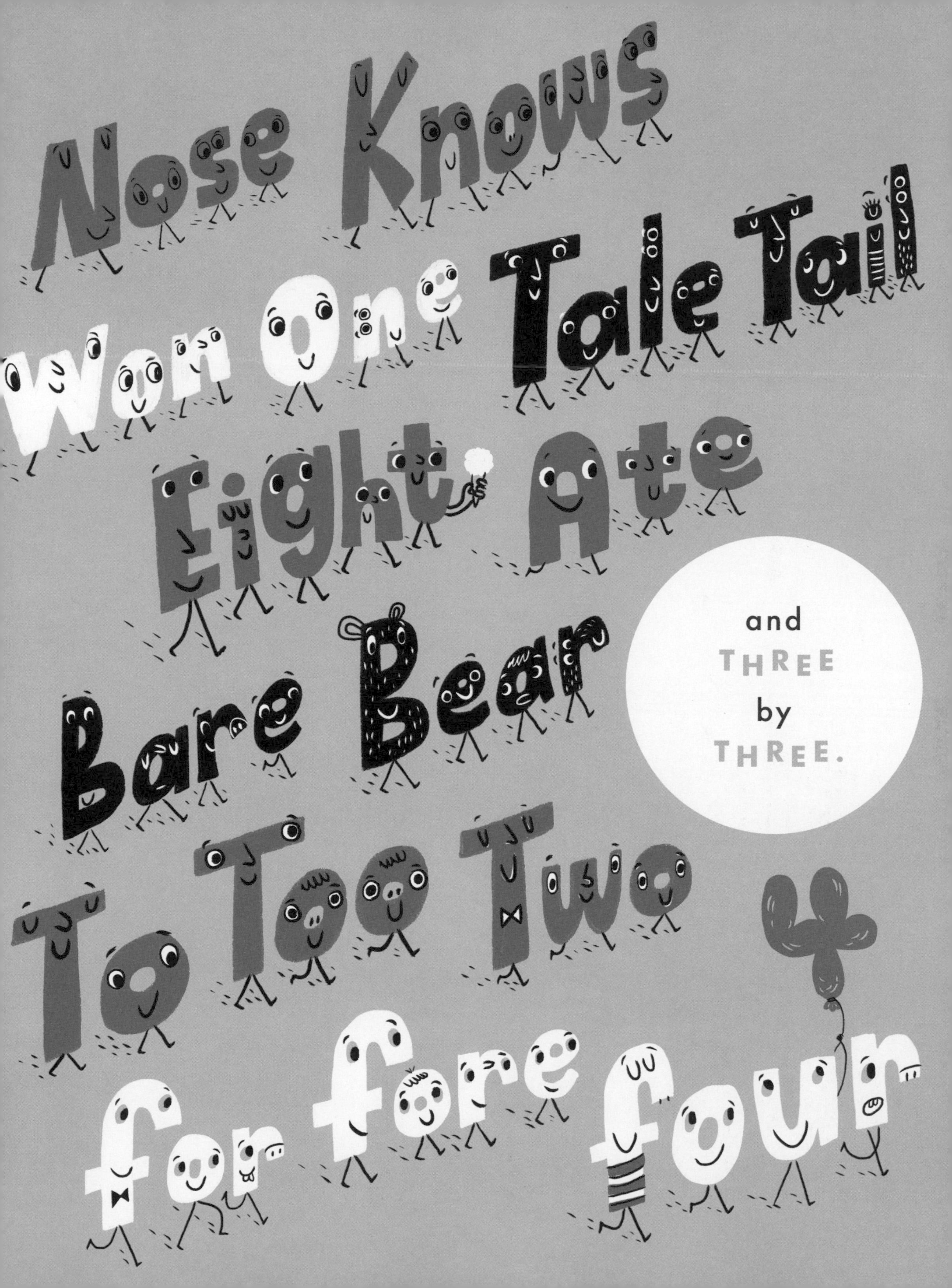
Nose Knows
Won One Tale Tail
Eight Ate
Bare Bear
To Too Two
for fore four
and
THREE
by
THREE.

Antonyms play **HIDE**-and-**SEEK**.

BIG
little

Attention! Attention! It's time for the PALINDROME family reunion.

HOLLYWORD BOWL

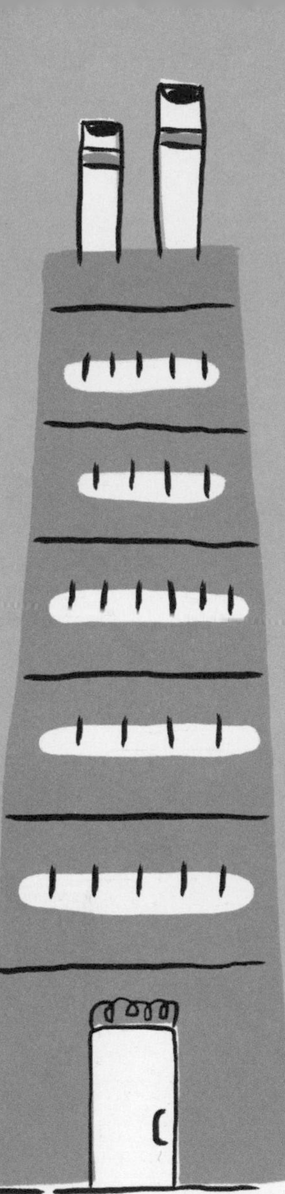

Archaic words strut their **SHAKESPEARE.**

Nuncle

Sneap

vizard

yerk

Proper nouns are **OH-SO-SPECIAL.**

Florida

Jabberwocky

Mars

Nile

SLIPPERY anagrams always amaze.

HEART

READ

EARTH

Fizzy
Dizzy
Tizzy

Ryhming words
hang out
TOGETHER.

Bird
Nerd
Word

fly

why

sky

Bunny

Sunny

Funny

Words with no RHYMES feel left out.

What's so special about rhyming?
Grrrr!
PENGUIN

HEY!
Huh?
Argh
Yay

Uh-oh!

Boo

Interjections INTERRUPT rudely.

D'oh!

Yippee!

Even the **CONJUNCTIONS** can't hold things together.

Boo
Unless
Yuck

Get back in the dictionary, all of you!
I
can't
Argh
No

WEBSTER'S
DICTIONARY
TOP
run

Escape
Wait for me!
Shhh.
ROGET'S THESAURUS
ROGET'S THESAURUS
Sometimes words spin out of control.
I say!
Yes. True. Verily. For example, my Synonyms seem to be plotting and scheming.

Skedaddle

This is fun!

Decamp

Powder

Glossary

PEOPLE

Noah Webster (1758–1843) Wrote the first dictionary of American English.

Peter Mark Roget (1779–1869) Created the most famous thesaurus of the English language

VOCABULARY

anagram Words or phrases that contain the same letters in a different order.

antonym A word that means the opposite of another word.

archaic Old-fashioned, not used anymore.

conjunction A word that connects words or phrases.

contraction Two words shortened and combined with an apostrophe.

garboil An old-fashioned word for confusion or turmoil.

homophones Words that sound alike but have different spellings.

interjection A word that expresses sudden emotion.

lexicon A dictionary.

nuncle An old-fashioned word for "uncle."

onomatopoeia A word that sounds like a natural noise.

palindrome A word or phrase that reads the same forward and backward.

pismire An old-fashioned word for "ant."

sackbut An old-fashioned trombone-like instrument.

sneap An old-fashioned word for "insult."

supercalifragilisticexpialidocious Extremely wonderful. (This extremely wonderful word is not yet included in every dictionary.)

synonym A word that means the same thing as another word.

thesaurus A book of synonyms and antonyms.

vizard An old-fashioned word for "mask."

yerk An old-fashioned word for "pull."